E FOS
Foster, Kelli C.
What a day for flying!

062509

GET READY...GET SET...READ!

WHAT A DAY FOR FLYING!

by
Foster & Erickson

Illustrations by
Kerri Gifford

BARRON'S

What a day for flying!

Trish was in her dish.
Pat had on her hat.

"Just look," said Trish.

"It is a dream come true."

Swish....
Pat's hat went flying off.

"Oh, no!" said Pat.
"There goes my hat."

Pat's hat went flying…

by Ned and Ted.

"Help," said Pat.
"Please get my hat."

Ned and Ted sped away
to get Pat's hat.

Pat's hat went flying
by the bug club.

It went flying by
slim Jim and the lop.

"Please," said Pat.
"Help get my hat."

Slim Jim, Ned, the lop,
and Ted all sped away
to get Pat's hat.

The fat rat and Ed
saw Pat's hat.

Pat's hat went down
with a plop and came to
a stop on the see-saw.

"Help, help," said Pat.
"Please get that hat."

But swish,
the hat went flying off.

Away they all sped—
slim Jim and Ned,
the lop and Ted,

the fat rat and Ed—
to get Pat's hat.

With a swish and a drop
the hat came to a stop
on top of Pop.

"Up there," said Pat.
"Let's get my hat."

Slim Jim and Ned,
the rat and Ed,
the lop and Ted,

and Trish and Pat
went up, up, up
to get Pat's hat.

"Tug, Pat, tug," they said.
And she did.

The hat went down,
and Pat went down.

They all went down
on top of Pat's hat.

Pat's hat was flat.

What a day for Pat's
flying hat!

DEAR PARENTS AND EDUCATORS:

Welcome to **Get Ready...Get Set...Read!**

We've created these books to introduce children to the magic of reading.

Each story in the series is built around one or two word families. For example, *A Mop for Pop* uses the OP word family. Letters and letter blends are added to OP to form words such as TOP, LOP, and STOP.

This **Bring-It-All-Together** book serves as a reading review. When your children have finished *Find Nat, The Sled Surprise, Sometimes I Wish, A Mop for Pop,* and *The Bug Club,* it is time to have them read this book. *What A Day for Flying* uses the characters and words introduced in the first five **Get Ready...Get Set...Read!** stories. (Each set in the series will be followed by two review books.)

Bring-It-All-Together books provide:
• much needed vocabulary repetition for developing fluency.
• longer stories for increasing reading attention spans.
• new stories with familiar characters for motivating young readers.

We have created these **Bring-It-All-Together** books to help develop confidence and competence in your young reader. We wish you much success in your reading adventures.

Kelli C. Foster, Ph.D.
Educational Psychologist

Gina Clegg Erickson, MA
Reading Specialist

© Copyright 1993 by Kelli C. Foster, Gina C. Erickson, and Kerri Gifford

All inquiries should be addressed to:
Barron's Educational Series, Inc.
250 Wireless Boulevard
Hauppauge, New York 11788

International Standard Book No. 0-8120-1557-6

Library of Congress Catalog Card No. 92-42078

Library of Congress Cataloging-in-Publication Data

Foster, Kelli C.
    What a day for flying! / by Foster & Erickson : illustrations by Kerri Gifford.
        p.   cm. — (Get ready—get set—read!)
    Summary: When Pat the cat's hat blows off her head while she and Trish the fish are flying in a hot air balloon, all of her friends join in pursuit of the hat as it flies around the countryside.
    ISBN 0-8120-1557-6
    (1. Cats—Fiction.   2. Hats—Fiction.   3. Animals—Fiction.)   I. Erickson, Gina Clegg.   II. Gifford, Kerri, ill.   III. Title.   IV. Series: Erickson, Gina Clegg. Get ready—get set—read!
PZ7.F8155Wh   1993
(E)—dc20
                                                            9242078
                                                               CIP
                                                               AC

PRINTED IN CHINA
19 18 17

There are five sets of books in the

Series. Each set consists of five **FIRST BOOKS** and two **BRING-IT-ALL-TOGETHER BOOKS**.

SET 1

is the first set your children should read.
The word families are selected from the short vowel sounds:
at, **ed**, **ish** and **im**, **op**, **ug**.

SET 2

provides more practice
with short vowel sounds:
an and **and**, **et**, **ip**, **og**, **ub**.

SET 3

focuses on
long vowel sounds:
ake, **eep**, **ide** and **ine**, **oke** and **ose**, **ue** and **ute**.

SET 4

introduces the idea that the word family sounds
can be spelled two different ways:
ale/ail, **een/ean**, **ight/ite**, **ote/oat**, **oon/une**.

SET 5

acquaints children with word families that
do not follow the rules for long and short vowel sounds:
all, **ound**, **y**, **ow**, **ew**.